Dog Knows Best

First published in 2007 by
Franklin Watts
338 Euston Road
London
NW1 3BH

Franklin Watts Australia
Level 17/207 Kent Street
Sydney
NSW 2000

Text © Margaret Nash 2007
Illustration © Peter Cottrill 2007

The rights of Margaret Nash to be identified as the author
and Peter Cottrill as the illustrator of this Work have
been asserted in accordance with the Copyright, Designs
and Patents Act, 1988.

A CIP catalogue record for this book is available
from the British Library.

ISBN 978 0 7496 7154 9 (hbk)
ISBN 978 0 7496 7297 3 (pbk)

Series Editor: Jackie Hamley
Series Advisor: Dr Hilary Minns
Series Designer: Peter Scoulding

Printed in China

Franklin Watts is a division of
Hachette Children's Books.

Dog Knows Best

by Margaret Nash

Illustrated by Peter Cottrill

W
FRANKLIN WATTS
LONDON•SYDNEY

Margaret Nash

"I don't have a dog. My cat is very clean and washes herself a lot. But I'm sure she would agree with Dog – baths are definitely to be avoided!"

Peter Cottrill

"I'm a bit of an old dog myself. I like a tasty biscuit, a good walk, a long sleep and someone to tell me: 'who's a clever boy'!"

Dog needed a wash.

"Put him in the bath," said Dad.

6

"Put him in the sink,"
said Jim.

But Dog did not
like that.

He zoomed from
the room.

He ran down the path.

He lay on the grass.

Dog peeped through
the fence and then he ..

... pushed through the bushes into next door's garden.

"Wuff!" said Dog.

Then ... squirt ... squirt!

Out came all the dirt!

"Dog knows best!"
laughed Dad.

Notes for adults

TADPOLES are structured to provide support for newly independent readers. The stories may also be used by adults for sharing with young children.

Starting to read alone can be daunting. **TADPOLES** help by providing visual support and repeating words and phrases. These books will both develop confidence and encourage reading and rereading for pleasure.

If you are reading this book with a child, here are a few suggestions:

1. Make reading fun! Choose a time to read when you and the child are relaxed and have time to share the story.

2. Talk about the story before you start reading. Look at the cover and the blurb. What might the story be about? Why might the child like it?

3. Encourage the child to reread the story, and to retell the story in their own words, using the illustrations to remind them what has happened.

4. Discuss the story and see if the child can relate it to their own experience, or perhaps compare it to another story they know.

5. Give praise! Remember that small mistakes need not always be corrected.

If you enjoyed this book,
why not try another TADPOLES story?

Sammy's Secret	Mop Top
978 0 7496 6890 7	978 0 7946 6895 2
Stroppy Poppy	Charlie and the Castle
978 0 7496 6893 8	978 0 7496 6896 9
I'm Taller Than You!	Over the Moon!
978 0 7496 6894 5	978 0 7496 6897 6
Leo's New Pet	My Sister is a Witch!
978 0 7496 6891 4	978 0 7496 6898 3